Children's Book Club Weekly Reader Children's Book Club Weekly Reader Children's Book Club Weekly Reader Children's Book Club Weekly Reader Children's Book Club Weekly Reader Children's Book Club Weekly Reader Children's Book Club Weekly Reader Children's Book Club Weekly Reader Children's Book Club Weekly Reader Children's Book Club Weekly Reader Children's Book Club Weekly Reader Children's Book Club Weekly Reader Children's Book Club Weekly Reader Children's Book Club Weekly Reader Children's Book Club Weekly Reader Children's Book Club Weekly Reader Children's Book Club Weekly Reader Children's Book Club Weekly Reader Children's Book Club Weekly Reader Children's Book Club Weekly Reader

THE ANIMALS WHO CHANGED THEIR COLORS

Library of Congress Cataloging in Publication Data

Allamand, Pascale.
    The animals who changed their colors.

    SUMMARY: The polar bear, whale, tortoise, and two
crocodiles try to imitate the parrot's beautiful colors,
only to discover how impractical they are.
    [1. Animals—Fiction.   2. Individuality—Fiction]
I. Title.
PZ7.A3987An 1979   [E]   79-196
ISBN 0-688-41900-3
ISBN 0-688-51900-8 lib. bdg.

Weekly Reader Children's Book Club presents

THE ANIMALS WHO CHANGED THEIR COLORS

PASCALE ALLAMAND

English version by ELIZABETH WATSON TAYLOR

Lothrop, Lee & Shepard Company
A Division of William Morrow & Co., Inc.
New York

A little bear lived on an iceberg. One day, he saw a big rainbow in the sky. He thought what fun it would be if he could change his white coat into a colored one.

He spoke to his friend the whale. She said she would like to change her color too. They decided to visit the lands where the animals have bright coats, to find out how they got them.

So they left the iceberg.
When the sun began to feel hot,
they traveled by night.

They landed on a pretty little beach.
A big tortoise came along
and the little bear and the whale
told her about their journey.
The tortoise asked if she could go
with them. She wanted to find herself
a nicer color too.

So they all three traveled on together.
They left the sea and went up a big river.
Sometimes it got very narrow.
Tall trees spread their branches
over the water. The whale could
only just squeeze through.

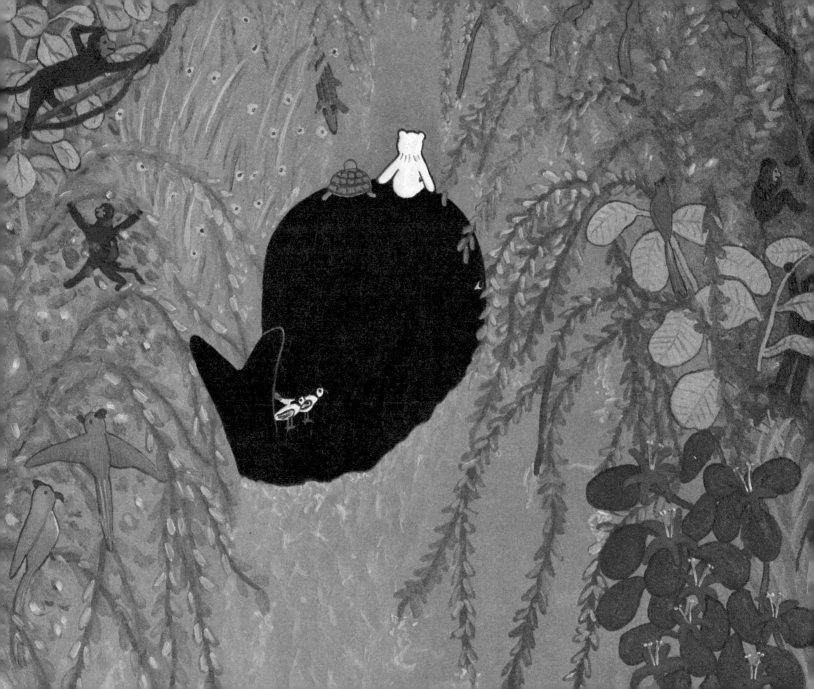

They met two crocodiles.
Their big teeth made the little bear
rather nervous so he stayed
on the whale's back to talk to them.
The crocodiles said they were tired of
being gray, and they asked to
go along as well.

Then the animals met a superb parrot.
They asked him what he did to be
so beautiful. He said he had done
nothing at all. He had been born
with colors that matched
the bright flowers of the jungle.

Next day, the whale went off on her own.
She found a pond full of red mud
and rolled in it till she was all red.
When she got back to her friends,
they admired her and asked
how she had done it. She told them.

The little bear rubbed himself
with leaves from a bush
till he was green. The crocodiles
rolled in some blue flowers, and soon
they were quite blue.

The tortoise found some pretty orange mushrooms. As she could not turn over on to her back, her friends rubbed her shell with mushrooms.

Very proud of their bright new colors, the animals began their journey home. When they met the parrot again, he told them they were silly to have changed their colors. His colors helped him hide from danger among the bright jungle flowers. He wanted to know where a red whale, green bear, orange tortoise, and two blue crocodiles would hide when they were back in their homes.

When they had thought about it,
the bear, the whale, the tortoise
and the crocodiles agreed that
the parrot was right.
So they decided to clean themselves
in the river.

The little bear and the whale
said goodbye to the crocodiles and
the tortoise, then they headed back to
the icebergs.

Back at home, the little bear
sometimes looks at himself in the water.
He wonders why he ever wanted
to change his beautiful white coat!